10 9 8 7 6 5 4 3 2 1 01 02 03 04 05

Printed in Mexico   49
First edition, November 2001
Book design by Nancy Goldenberg
The text of this book is set in 20 point Jacoby ICG Black.
The illustrations are acrylic.

Library of Congress Cataloging-in-Publication Data
Greene, Rhonda Gowler.
Jamboree Day / by Rhonda Gowler Greene ; illustrated by Jason Wolff.
p.   cm.
Summary: All the animals in the jungle have a grand time at the annual Jamboree Day.
ISBN 0-439-29310-3 (alk. paper)
[1. Jungle animals—Fiction. 2. Parties—Fiction. 3. Stories in rhyme.] I. Wolff, Jason, ill. II. Title.
PZ8.3.G824 Jam 2001 [E]—dc21   00-66589

Jamboree Day

by **Rhonda Gowler Greene**

illustrated by **Jason Wolff**

Orchard Books   New York • **An Imprint of Scholastic Inc.**

Deep in the jungle every middle of May
there's a big celebration called Jamboree Day,
when the animals come from all around
to dance and party to a jamboree sound.

Little Tree Frog woke that morning in May
and readied himself for Jamboree Day.
Then he hip-hop-hurried round far and near
to tell everyone the day was here.

"Now scrub your necks and shine your shoes
and call your cousins and spread the news!"

Word took wing on the jungle breeze
and floated from the valleys to the tops of the trees.
All the animals couldn't wait to come
to the annual jungle jamboree fun!

The first to arrive were the Cheetah twins,
bouncing to the plinking of their mandolins.
Next came Giraffe and Zebra too,
the Aardvark family and their neighbor, Gnu.

Lion showed up wearing his best,
in tie and tails, like an honored guest.
Gorilla gathered all of his kin.
Chattering chimps *swooosh!*-swung right in.

Ants came marching. Eland leapt.
Leopard jogged in. Lizard crept.
Flamingo flew in just in time.
Python *s-s-s-slithered* down a vine.

Splish!-ing, *splash!*-ing up the muddy Nile
came Mr. and Mrs. Crocodile.
"Everyone's here!" clucked the Cuckoo clan.
"Time to begin!" And the jamboree began!

Coconut milk was the jamboree drink.
Old friends toasted. Glasses clinked.
Banana splits were served all around.
Tickets sold out for the merry-go-round.

The jamboree train chugged round its track
with a *choo-choo-choo* and a *clackity-clack*.
Balloons were sold for a teeny, tiny dime.
Everyone was having such a wonderful time!

Parrot Pete mimicked Hollywood stars
with their fancy "do's" and their fancy cars.
Hyena laughed till his sides were sore.
The audience shouted, "More! Encore!"

Hippo twirled on her tip-tippy toes,
while Frog slip-slid down Elephant's nose.
Spider tapped on eight hairy legs.
Rhinoceros juggled ostrich eggs.

The limbo game was hard to do,
but not for some. Can you guess who?
The waterfall ride was a favorite spot
where the animals headed when it got too hot.

Bands played bebop, blues, and jazz
with a *toot-toot-tootle* and a *razzmatazz*.
Everyone jitterbugged, boogied, and bopped
and wiggled and jiggled till the music stopped.

Then . . . sun sank low. Shadows fell.
The jungle climbed out of its jamboree spell.

With happy hugs and warm good-byes,
the animals left, sighing jamboree sighs . . .

while Frog hip-hopped from ear to ear,
whispering to all, "Hope to see you next year!"